A NOTE TO PARENTS

When your children are ready to "step into reading," giving them the right books is as crucial as giving them the right food to eat. **Step into Reading Books** present exciting stories and information reinforced with lively, colorful illustrations that make learning to read fun, satisfying, and worthwhile. They are priced so that acquiring an entire library of them is affordable. And they are beginning readers with a difference—they're written on five levels.

Early Step into Reading Books are designed for brand-new readers, with large type and only one or two lines of very simple text per page. **Step 1 Books** feature the same easy-to-read type as the Early Step into Reading Books, but with more words per page. **Step 2 Books** are both longer and slightly more difficult, while **Step 3 Books** introduce readers to paragraphs and fully developed plot lines. **Step 4 Books** offer exciting nonfiction for the increasingly independent reader.

The grade levels assigned to the five steps—preschool through kindergarten for the Early Books, preschool through grade 1 for Step 1, grades 1 through 3 for Step 2, grades 2 through 3 for Step 3, and grades 2 through 4 for Step 4—are intended only as guides. Some children move through all five steps very rapidly; others climb the steps over a period of several years. Either way, these books will help your child "step into reading" in style!

W9-BGQ-553

For Colin and Patrick Ruel:
Keep your eye on the ball.

Text copyright © 1998 by Jon Buller and Susan Schade. All rights reserved under International and Pan-American Copyright Conventions. Published in the United States by Random House, Inc., New York, and simultaneously in Canada by Random House of Canada Limited, Toronto.

http://www.randomhouse.com/

Library of Congress Cataloging-in-Publication Data
Buller, Jon, 1943–
Baseball camp on the planet of the eyeballs / Jon Buller and Susan Schade.
p. cm. — (A step 3 book) SUMMARY: On his way to baseball camp, a young boy is zapped to the Planet of the Eyeballs, where he teaches the inhabitants to play ball.
ISBN 0-679-88737-7 (pbk.) — ISBN 0-679-98737-1 (lib. bdg.)
[1. Baseball—Fiction. 2. Camps—Fiction. 3. Fantasy.] I. Title. II. Series: Step into reading book.
Step 3 book. PZ7.B9135Bas 1998 [E]—dc21 97-23475

Printed in the United States of America 10 9 8 7 6 5 4 3 2 1

STEP INTO READING is a registered trademark of Random House, Inc.

Step into Reading®

BASEBALL CAMP
ON THE
PLANET OF THE EYEBALLS

By Jon Buller
and Susan Schade

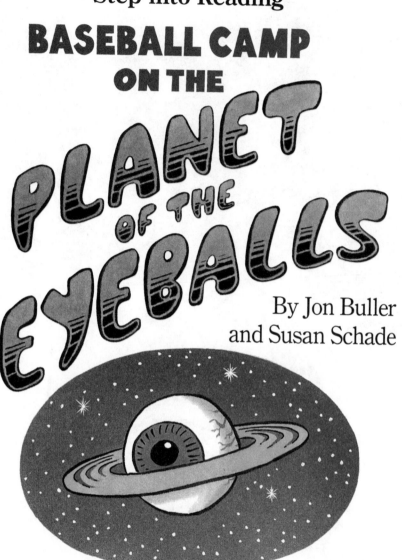

A Step 3 Book

Random House New York

August 15, 4:10 p.m.
Memorial Field, Boxton

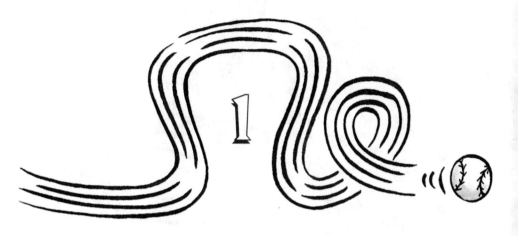

It was the bottom of the sixth and the score was 0–0.

I was the next batter up for Spinnato's Beauty Salon.

I was excited.

Our rivals, Dave's Seafood Shack, were undefeated. But today they hadn't scored.

We still had a chance! If only we could get a run...

I stepped up to the plate.

The pitcher for Dave's Seafood was
Dan Ditko. He was the reason they were
undefeated. No kid in Regional Little
League had been able to hit his incredible
fastball.

I squinted at him and raised my bat. I
was ready. And I had an idea.

I was going to start my swing *before*
he actually threw the ball!

I watched his windup...The left foot off
the ground...The right arm behind the
head...The left foot making a little circle
in the air...

I started my swing.

SMACK!!! The ball and bat connected with a jolt that set my teeth rattling. I dropped the bat and stood there, dazed.

The crowd roared! Dan Ditko was in shock. The coach was waving at me—go! go!

I started running toward first base.

A hit! I had hit a Dan Ditko pitch!

I rounded second.

Coach waved me on. "All the way, Hugo!" he yelled. "It's a homer!"

I headed for home plate.

"*HU-GO! HU-GO! HU-GO!*" The fans were shouting my name.

It was the greatest day of my life!

August 16, 8:55 a.m.
Boxton Bus Station

2

It was the day after my big game.

I was on my way to baseball camp for a week. And when I got back, we would have another chance to beat Dave's Seafood—in the championship!

My parents drove me to the bus terminal.

I said, "You can let me out here."

My mother knows I don't like her kissing me in front of the other kids, but sometimes she can't help herself. Besides, I wanted to take off the dorky-looking sweater she had made me wear over my uniform.

I waved good-bye and ducked into the men's bathroom.

I took off the sweater and stuffed it into my duffel bag. Then I put on the cool lightning bolt baseball cap that Dan Ditko had given me.

He had surprised me after my homer by coming over to shake my hand. "Good hit, Hugo," he had said. And he had given me the cap he used to wear around school!

I picked up my bag and grinned at myself in the mirror. "Home run king!" I said softly.

Suddenly a bright light surrounded me. My skin tingled, and I felt strangely weightless. I started to rise up off the ground! I could see myself in the mirror, floating helplessly, up and up and up.

I tried to cry out, but the only sound I could make was a little gurgle in my throat.

Then I disappeared right through the ceiling of the men's bathroom!

The next thing I knew, I was inside a spaceship, surrounded by skinny-legged *eyeballs!* They were staring at me and beeping.

"Ma!" I cried. "Dad! HELP!"

The eyeballs stopped beeping. They looked at each other. One of them stepped forward and spoke to me in English.

"Don't worry, Agent 86. You may have gone so far into your undercover identity on Earth that you have forgotten your own language. We have heard of this happening before. When we get home and you morph into your own shape, it will come back to you."

I looked behind me, but there was nobody there. The eyeball was talking to *me!*

I said, "But I'm not Agent 86! I don't know what you're talking about! I'm Hugo

LaRosa, of 47 Mallow Vine Lane, on my way to baseball camp! You're making a terrible mistake!"

August 16, 6:35 p.m.
Planet of the Eyeballs

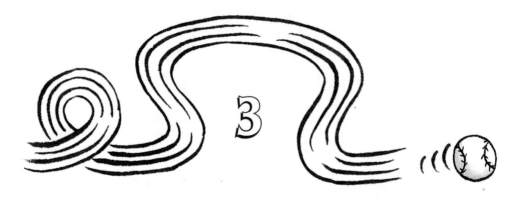

They didn't believe me, but at least they left me alone.

Hours later we landed on a small, bare planet.

They walked me to a little round house, called a pod, and fed me some horrible glop. Then they sat down and waited for me to morph back into an eyeball. They told me that I—Agent 86— was expected to make an important report about Earth to the Chief Eyeball Official.

"But I'm *not* Agent 86!" I said. "I'm Hugo LaRosa, and I'm not morphing into anything or anybody else!"

On the second day they said that the Chief Eyeball Official was demanding to hear my report, and they might have to use forced morphing to get me to cooperate!

That got me worried. Forced morphing? Not if I could help it! I said, "All right, I'll make a report—but only if I can do it in human form."

They agreed. I took my duffel bag in case they wanted to send me home afterward, and I followed them to a huge arena.

The Chief Eyeball Official (otherwise known as the CEO) was waiting for me. The other eyeballs sat in the stands and watched.

"Uh...well..." I didn't know what to say.

Then I remembered my third-grade teacher, Mr. Morgan, telling me to write about what I knew. So what did I know?

"Baseball," I said.

"What?" said the CEO.

"Uh...life on Earth is sort of like baseball," I said.

The CEO waited.

"Baseball is a game played on a ball field with two teams," I said. "There are nine players on each team. One team stands in the field. Their pitcher throws the ball, and the batter on the other team tries to hit it."

Once I got going, it wasn't so hard. I guess Mr. Morgan was right.

"When the batter hits the ball," I continued, "he gets to run around the bases and score."

After I had finished, the CEO looked at me for a long time. Finally he said, "I don't get it."

August 17, 1:15 p.m.
Eyeball Stadium

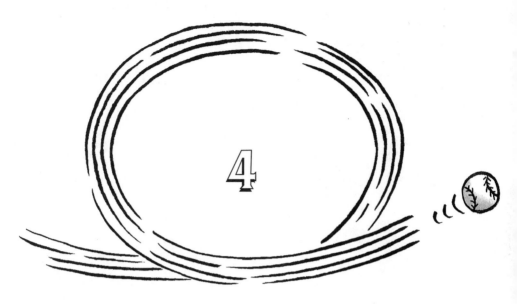

How could I explain?

I took my bat and ball out of my duffel bag.

I said, "This is the bat, and this is the ball."

"Good, good!" said the CEO. "We will have a demonstration!" He beeped at the stands, and eighteen eyeballs came down to play baseball.

They looked at me, waiting for instructions. I looked at them.

"Uh...it's easier to play if you have arms," I said.

The eighteen eyeballs beeped among themselves for a minute. Then they morphed into Hugo LaRosas! They all looked exactly like me!

I said we needed to be able to tell the two teams apart by having different uniforms or something.

The CEO smiled. He zapped one team with a glance, and they all turned blue. Then he zapped the other team, and they all turned pink. It was the Pinks against the Blues.

I told everyone where to stand. I showed the Pink pitcher how to throw the ball. I showed the Blue batter how to swing the bat.

"Batter up! Play ball!"

The Pink pitcher threw the ball.

The Blue batter waited, ready to swing. But just before the ball reached home plate, it swerved and took off in another direction.

The batter chased after it, swinging at it with the bat. The eyeballs in the stands laughed and cheered.

"STOP!" I yelled. "What's going on here?"

The CEO explained it to me. The pitcher was using thought waves to control the ball.

"That's cheating," I said. "You just throw the ball and take your chances."

The Blue batter hit the next pitch. A grounder to third base.

"Good!" I yelled. "Batter, run to first! Third baseman..."

I stared. The ball had stopped in mid-bounce right in front of the third baseman. It hovered there while he waited to hear my instructions.

I sighed and looked at the CEO. "Thought waves?" I asked.

He nodded. "It's natural for them," he said. "They will try to hide it from you, but they probably won't stop. If you see the red glint in their eyes, you'll know they are controlling the ball. The only way to be sure they don't cheat is to bring out a thought wave inhibitor."

The players groaned.

An eyeball was sent out and came back with a big magnet. He set it down behind home plate.

So *that's* a thought wave inhibitor, I thought. It looked like a regular old magnet to me.

The game went pretty smoothly after that.

The eyeballs in the stands were soon going wild. I was surprised to see that they had divided into two groups. On one side, they cheered and gave off a pink glow whenever the Pinks hit the ball. On the other side, they cheered and gave off a blue glow whenever the Blues got a hit.

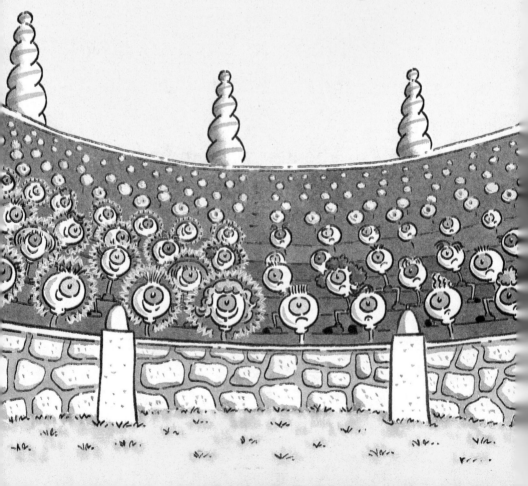

I pointed this out to the CEO.

He nodded and said, "I think I am beginning to understand life on Earth."

I thought it might be a good time to ask him to send me home. I explained about the championship game coming up in five days, and I told him how my team needed me to beat Dave's Seafood.

"Don't be silly," he said. "What could be more important than the Pinks and the Blues? We will have another game tomorrow!"

August 18, 3:50 p.m.
Eyeball Stadium

What could I do?

We played baseball every day for the next four days. We practiced throwing and running and batting. In fact, it was pretty much like baseball camp. Except that I was miserable. And usually I *love* baseball camp!

I kept worrying about forced morphing. And about what my parents would do when I didn't show up at the bus terminal. They would never find me *here!* And what about the big championship game?

One small eyeball had become our bat boy. I liked him because he called me Hugo instead of Agent 86. I called him Bat Boy.

Bat Boy told me that he hoped to be sent on a fact-finding mission to Earth someday. I said he should look me up when he got there. He said he would.

I told him all about Dan Ditko and my big home run, and how much I wanted to play in the championship game.

He looked around. Then he whispered, "Maybe it could be arranged."

I stared at him. "What? An escape?"

"Shhh."

We met after practice to make our plans. Was it a mistake for me to trust such a small eyeball? I didn't know. But it was my only hope.

I left all the technical stuff to Bat Boy. He *said* he knew how to pilot a flying saucer.

He told me to meet him on the roof of my pod at midnight.

I climbed up. It was dark, but the eyeballs had built-in headlights, so I could see them moving around on the bare landscape.

By midnight they had all gone inside their pods.

I waited...

One minute. Two minutes. Five minutes.

The flying saucer approached silently. I didn't even see it until it was almost on top of me. Then the hatch opened and a rope ladder was lowered.

Bat Boy apologized for the ladder. "I didn't want to beam you up in case somebody saw the light," he said.

He focused his eye on the dials. I saw the telltale red glint of thought waves. The flying saucer hummed. We were heading for Earth!

"Won't they come after us?" I asked.

"I don't think so. I left a note for my father. I said that I was sure you weren't Agent 86, and that we were going back to find the real one."

"Oh," I said. "You have a father?"

"Of course. He's the CEO."

Suddenly I felt a little better about hurtling through space with a small eyeball. At least he was the son of the Chief Eyeball Official!

About twelve hours later, Bat Boy landed the flying saucer in the woods behind the bus terminal.

I checked my watch. It was 11:55 a.m., and my parents were meeting the noon bus. "Wow!" I said. "Good timing!"

Bat Boy smiled and scuffed his feet. He said, "I'll see you at the big game."

August 22, 12:00 noon
Boxton Bus Station

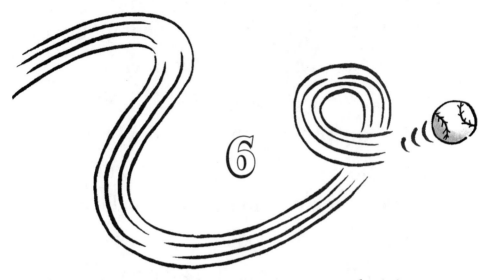

My parents were happy to see me, but not as happy as I was to see *them!* My mother said, "So how was baseball camp?"

"Uh...okay."

My mother smiled at my father. "He's exhausted, poor thing."

She was right. I fell asleep in the car.

The next thing I knew I was in my own bed, and they were shaking me awake. "It's three-thirty. Time to get ready for the championship game!"

Right from the start the game did not go well.

I had told my team about swinging early against Dan Ditko, but it wasn't working. We were down, 2–0.

The top of the fifth. I was the first batter up. I swung early, but the ball slowed down and I missed it. "Strike one!"

The next pitch looked good. I swung, but at the last second the ball curved right up over my bat. "Strike two!"

Third pitch. I watched Dan Ditko. He must have learned some new tricks in baseball camp. The windup. The pitch.

And then I saw it. A glint of red light in Dan Ditko's eyes! The unmistakable sign of thought waves!

I gasped. *Dan Ditko was Agent 86!* In a flash it all became clear to me! His ball control! Even his lightning bolt cap! He had wanted me out of the way, so he gave me his cap, and that's why the eyeballs picked *me* up!

I was so surprised, I didn't even swing. "Strike three! You're out!"

I ran over to my parents in the stands. "You've gotta do something for me, *please!* It's crucial! Go home and get all the magnets from the refrigerator, and *hurry!*"

"Hugo, whatever for?"

"I can't explain! There's no time. I need them before the start of the sixth inning. *Run!*"

In the sixth inning I stood as near home plate as I could get. My pockets were full of refrigerator magnets, and they were working!

Dan Ditko walked the first three batters. Finally he managed to get a slow one over the plate—and Ramona Spinnato belted it for a grand slam!

Dave's Seafood fell apart. We won the championship, 26–2.

I met Dan Ditko as he was being led off the field by a short kid with big eyes—Bat Boy in human form!

"Thanks a lot, Hugo!" Dan snarled. "If it wasn't for you, I could have been the youngest kid ever to make the majors!"

"Yeah? Well, that's not the way we play the game," I said to Dan.

I shook Bat Boy's hand and thanked him for believing in me. He winked and said, "I'll be back, Hugo. If you want to get in touch with me, just put on that lightning bolt cap. It transmits thought-wave mail. So long!"

I watched them walk away. "Thought-wave mail?" I said to myself. "Cool!"